EDITORIAL BY ERIC GERON

PRINTED IN THE UNITED STATES OF AMERICA
FIRST PAPERBACK EDITION, APRIL 2018
1 3 5 7 9 10 8 6 4 2

ISBN 978-1-4847-9968-0
FAC-029261-18047
LIBRARY OF CONGRESS CONTROL NUMBER: 2017961373

JOKES BY STEVE BEHLING

WITH HELP FROM EMMY CICIEREGA

DISNEY PRESS

LOS ANGELES · NEW YORK

THE KIDS

MR. McDEE

~~INTRODUCTION~~
iNTRO-**DUCK**-tiON!

> THIS NOTEPAD IS THE
> PROPERTY OF
> LAUNCHPAD
> MCQUACK

TESTING! TESTING! i BOUGHT THiS NOTEPAD TO WRiTE DOWN SOME JOKES i'VE BEEN WORKiNG ON.

COMEDY iS A BiG PART OF MY LiFE! iT'S GOTTEN ME OUT OF SOME PRETTY TOUGH SPOTS iN THE PAST. iS SOMEONE MAD AT YOU FOR CRASHiNG YOUR LiMO iNTO HiS iN-GROUND POOL? CRACK A JOKE LiKE "THAT'S **ONE** WAY TO WASH YOUR CAR!" AND SOMETiMES ALL iS FORGiVEN! SOMETiMES.

PRETTY MUCH EVERYONE LOVES MY JOKES, ESPECiALLY MY PALS HUEY, DEWEY, LOUiE, AND WEBBY!

BUT THERE'S ONE PERSON i'VE NEVER BEEN ABLE TO MAKE LAUGH, AND THAT'S MY BOSS, MR. MCDEE. i JUST **KNOW** THERE'S A FUNNY BONE iN THAT GUY! iM GONNA QUACK HiM UP!

ugh. I seriously doubt it!

JOKES TO TRY ON SCROOGE

WHAT DO YOU CALL iT
WHEN YOU CAN'T
RECOVER THE TREASURE?

MiSS-FORTUNE.

WHAT WILL DONALD INHERIT FROM SCROOGE?

A BAD TEMPER.

It's true. I've written him out of the will several times this week.

WHY DOES SCROOGE TAKE **BATHS** iN HiS MONEY?

BECAUSE HE'S **FiLTHY RiCH.**

WHERE DOES A VAMPiRE KEEP HER MONEY?

iN A BLOOD BANK.

WHY WAS THE
MILLIONAIRE UPSET?

HE USED TO BE A
BILLIONAIRE.

This isn't funny—
IT'S _TERRIFYING!_

SCROOGE LiKES HiS TEA
LiKE HE LiKES HiS MONEY:

GREEN, FRESHLY MiNTED,
AND iN BAGS.

Not true.

I like my tea
with an old tea
bag to save
money, a drop
of milk, and a
hint of nutmeg.

AH, RiGHT! YOU'D THiNK i'D
KNOW THAT BY NOW. YOU ALWAYS
SPiLL iT iN THE LiMO WHEN i
MAKE A SHARP TURN.

Have you ever made a soft turn?

NOT VERY SOFTEN!

WHAT'S WHITE AND PINK AND LEAVES YOU BLACK AND BLUE?

WEBBY IN A FIGHT!

Sorry, Launchpad!
Don't sneak up on me
next time!

HOW DO YOU MAKE A JOKE LAND WELL?

PLEASE DON'T ASK ME.
i CAN'T LAND ANYTHING **WELL!**

↖ case in point!

WHAT'S MORE VALUABLE THAN GOLD?

~~YOUR FRIENDSHIP, MR. MCDEE.~~ 😊

Diamonds.

IF THERE WERE A TV SHOW
ABOUT OUR ADVENTURES,
WHAT GENRE WOULD IT BE?

DUCKUMENTARY.

WHAT IS DEWEY'S
FAVORITE MELON?

HONEYDEWEY.

WHY DID DONALD TAKE A JOB BABYSITTING A BABOON?

HE NEEDED THE <u>MONKEY</u>.

WHAT DO YOU CALL A TEN-FOOT-TALL DUCK?

HUGE-Y.

We have some jokes, too, Launchpad!

What did the waiter say to the duck?

Waddle you have to eat?

← NICE!

Why did Donald's houseboat sink?

It hit a Duckburg.

← HA!

What do you call a duck who's always hungry?

Lunchpad. iT's TRUE!

HEY! WHY DOESN'T ANYONE BUT ME WEAR PANTS?

NO, REALLY, i'M TRYING TO FiGURE THiS OUT. PLEASE TELL ME. THERE'S NO PUNCH LiNE HERE.

I'm not laughing. Not even a little.

WHAT'S HUEY, DEWEY, AND LOUIE'S FAVORITE FOOD?

QUACKARONI AND CHEESE!

(IT'S MINE, TOO, IF I'M BEING HONEST.)

WHICH DUCK IS A GREAT BASKETBALL PLAYER?

DONALD **DUNK.**

WHY CAN'T YOU **FEED** A TEDDY BEAR?

iT'S ALREADY **STUFFED.**

WHY DIDN'T THE **SHARK EAT THE CLOWN?**

HE TASTED **FUNNY.**

WHY DOES GLOMGOLD
WEAR TWO KILTS WHEN HE
GOES GOLFING?

IN CASE HE
GETS A
HOLE
IN ONE.

WHY IS DUCKWORTH
BAD AT LYING?

YOU CAN
SEE RIGHT
THROUGH
HIM!

*This is all
a bunch of
nonsense!*

I got another one! What's the difference between Launchpad and a garbage can?

They both kind of smell and are pretty hollow inside. . . . Is it that the can is made out of metal?

Launchpad <u>can</u> crash; the <u>can</u> holds trash.

What's seven feet tall, covered in white fur, and growling?

Uncle Donald's alter ego?

I don't know. Why do you ask?

Because it's standing right behind you!

What gets wetter the more it dries?

Oh! Let me check my Junior Woodchucks Guide!

The idea of money evaporating and making me cry?

A TOWEL!

THANKS, KIDS. BUT SCROOGE STILL ISN'T LAUGHING. LET ME GIVE IT ANOTHER GO.

WHAT GOES UP BUT NEVER COMES DOWN?

A DUCK'S AGE!

HOW MANY DUCKS ARE IN DUCKBURG?

ONE!

(THINK ABOUT IT. . . .)

WHAT DO YOU SEE TWICE A WEEK, ONCE A YEAR, BUT NEVER IN A DAY?

Launchpad, some of your "jokes" hurt my head.

THE LETTER E!

A DUCK, A GOOSE, AND A MONKEY ARE CLIMBING TO THE TOP OF A COCONUT TREE. WHO WILL GET THE BANANA FIRST—THE DUCK, THE GOOSE, OR THE MONKEY?

The duck, if she's got a grappling hook!

NO<u>BODY</u>—YOU CAN'T GET A BANANA FROM A COCONUT TREE.

Hey! That was a trick!

Why can't your bicycle stand up?

It's <u>two tired</u>.

Can I retire to my study now?

<u>RE-TIRE?!</u> GOOD ONE,
SCROOGE! I SEE WHAT YOU
DID THERE! I BET YOU'RE
<u>WHEEL</u>-Y TIRED.

Are we done here?

WHAT HAS EiGHTY-EiGHT KEYS
BUT CAN'T OPEN A LOCK?

Scrooge!

He has a whole key ring and won't
open certain doors in his mansion!

A PiANO.

WHiCH WEiGHS MORE: A
POUND OF FEATHERS
OR A POUND OF GOLD?

NEiTHER. THEY <u>BOTH</u>
WEiGH A POUND.

Here's one!

Launchpad was driving a truck. He didn't have his lights on. There was no moon. Donald crossed the street in front of him. How did Launchpad see Donald?

IT WAS A SUNNY DAY!

WHAT DO YOU BREAK EVERY TIME YOU SAY IT?

SILENCE.

Oh, snap. That was good.

Hey, what word starts with an E and ends with an E but only has one letter in it?

"Envelope"!

You're in a dark cave. You have a candle, a lamp, and a torch. What do you light first?

Whatever casts the brightest light!

A match!

THERE'S A JOKE ON
THE NEXT PAGE
SO FUNNY,
SO HYSTERICAL
YOU MAY NEVER STOP
LAUGHING!

I seriously doubt that.

GROSS
JOKES

OKAY, HERE GOES:
WHICH NEPHEW LOVES TO SPIT?

LOOGie.

↳ That was pretty good!

WHY WOULDN'T THE MUMMY
LEAVE THE PYRAMID?

HE DIDN'T
HAVE THE
GUTS.

When do you know your room is too dirty?

 When the bugs leave a sign that says "Clean me!"

How do you make
a tissue dance?

Put a little
BOOGIE in it!

WHAT'S YELLOW AND
STICKY AND SMELLS LIKE
A BANANA?

MONKEY SNOT.

WHICH NEPHEW HATES
TO TAKE A BATH?

PEE-YEW-Y.

WHAT'S GREEN AND STICKS
TO THE BOTTOM OF A
DUCK'S FOOT?

A SQUASHED FROG.

WHAT DO YOU CALL A PAIR
OF SPATS THAT SCROOGE
KEEPS IN HIS BILL?

SPITS.

*I WOULD
NEVER.*

WHAT'S GROSSER THAN A
DUCK WHO DROOLS IN HIS
DINNER?

A DUCK WHO DROOLS IN
YOUR DINNER.

Why does Louie
chew food and talk
at the same time?

He likes to "show and tell."

What can I say? I love
see-food!

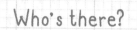

KNOCK KNOCK.

Who's there?

BUTTER.

Butter WHO?

BUTTER LET ME IN,
IT'S COLD OUT HERE!

KNOCK KNOCK.

Who's there?

A DUCK SAYS.

A duck says who?

NO, A DUCK SAYS
"QUACK." AN OWL SAYS
"WHO"!

Knock knock.

WHO'S THERE?

Figs,

FIGS WHO?

Figs

the plane so we can go home!

OKAY, OKAY!
I WAS BUSY WRITING
KNOCK-KNOCK JOKES.

KNOCK KNOCK.

Who's there?

A DUCK.

A duck who?

A DUCK WHO LOVES KNOCK-KNOCK JOKES, OBVIOUSLY!

KNOCK KNOCK.

Who's there?

TREE.

Tree who?

TREE
NEPHEWS.

KNOCK KNOCK.

Who's there?

HUEY, DEWEY, AND LOUIE.

Huey, Dewey, and Louie who?

Don't you remember your own nephews?!

Knock knock.

WHO'S THERE?

Knock knock.

WHO'S THERE?!

Knock knock.

WHO'S THERE?!?

Huey,
Dewey,
and Louie.

I got one more!

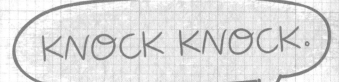

KNOCK KNOCK.

WHO'S THERE?

NOBODY.

NOBODY WHO?

NOBODY YET! WEBBY
RIGHT OVER!

Ri-DUCK-ULOUS

HOW DO YOU MAKE AN EGG QUACK?

BWEAK iT OPEN.

~~~~~~

WHY DOES DONALD LiVE ON A HOUSEBOAT?

~~~~~~

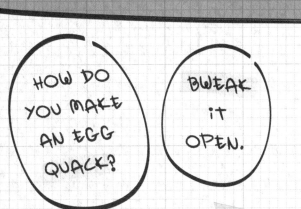

BECAUSE iF YOU PUT A REGULAR HOUSE iN THE WATER, iT WOULD SiNK.

WHAT DOES
MRS. BEAKLEY USE
TO FLIP PANCAKES?

JUDO.

WHY DID THE BEAGLE
BOYS TAKE A BATH?

SO THEY COULD MAKE A
CLEAN ESCAPE.

Does your shirt have any holes in it?

No.

Then how did you put it on?

Why do I have to go to bed every night?

Because the bed won't come to you!

That dog has no nose.

How does he smell?

Awful!

Why does Launchpad
fly a plane?

Because his arms are
TIRED.

WHAT DO YOU CALL AN EIGHT-LEGGED DUCK?

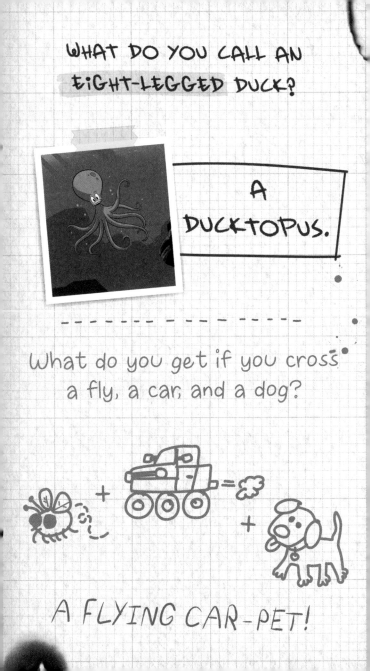

A DUCKTOPUS.

What do you get if you cross a fly, a car, and a dog?

A FLYING CAR-PET!

Why does Launchpad keep
his music player in the
refrigerator?

So he can
listen to some
cool music.

WHAT'S THE END OF EVERYTHING?

G.

WHAT'S FASTER—
HOT OR COLD?

HOT.
YOU CAN CATCH COLD.

What do you get if you cross a
snake and a kangaroo?

A JUMP
ROPE!

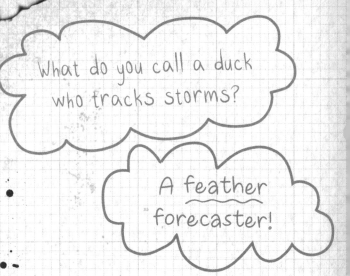

What do you call a duck who tracks storms?

A feather forecaster!

WHAT DO YOU CALL A DUCK WHO FLIES A PLANE AND IS YOUR BEST FRIEND?

LAUNCHPAL.

WHY WOULDN'T THE DUCK WEAR THE ROOSTER COSTUME?

She didn't want anyone to think she was <u>chicken</u>.

Why wouldn't the duck pay for dinner?

The bill was too much.

What's green and dizzy and has webbed feet?

A seasick duck.

Also known as me when we go in the submarine. Blegh!

WHAT HAS FEATHERS AND LEADS AN ORCHESTRA?

A CON-DUCK-TOR!

How do you catch a unique duck?

EASY. UNIQUE UP ON HER.

HOW DO YOU STICK TWO DUCKS TOGETHER?

WITH DUCK TAPE!

How many of these jokes are based on real-life Donald mishaps?

A LOT!
HE'S MY MUSE.

He's a-musing, all right!

HOW MANY DUCKS CAN YOU
SQUEEZE INTO A BARREL?

ABOUT THREE BEFORE
IT QUACKS.

HOW DID THE DUCK
GET INTO A JAM?

SHE FELL INTO A VAT
OF STRAWBERRIES.

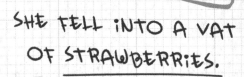

WHAT DO DUCKS LIKE TO EAT FOR LUNCH?

CHEESE AND QUACKERS.

WHY DID THE DUCK GO TO THE BANK?

SHE WANTED TO GET A NEW BILL.

$ $

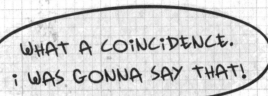

QUACK! QUACK!

WHAT A COINCIDENCE. i WAS GONNA SAY THAT!

WHAT DID THE MAMA DUCK SAY TO HER EGG?

HATCH YOU LATER.

Whose mother? What egg?

ADVENTURE

WHAT SHOULD YOU DO iF YOU FALL iNTO A SHARK'S MOUTH?

Try not to smell its breath.

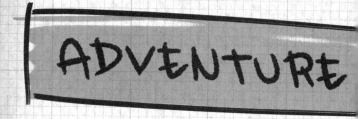

What do you call a giant glacier monster?

ANYTHING iT WANTS. 😊

What should you do if you're frozen in a block of ice?

KEEP COOL.

THERE'S A SECRET LAB WITH FOUR WALLS. THE WALLS ALL FACE SOUTH. THERE'S A BEAR OUTSIDE. WHAT KIND OF BEAR IS IT?

A POLAR BEAR!

(IF ALL THE WALLS ARE FACING SOUTH, THEN THE LAB IS AT THE NORTH POLE.)

This isn't even a polar bear!

WHAT'S THE BEST WAY TO CLIMB MOUNT NEVERREST?

PRACTICE!

How many jewels can you put in an empty backpack?

One. As soon as you put it in, the backpack's not empty!

WHAT SCHOOL DO YOU HAVE TO DROP OUT OF BEFORE YOU CAN GRADUATE?

PARACHUTE SCHOOL!

HOW DO YOU MAKE A SUBMARINE SINK?

PUT A SINK IN A SUBMARINE.

WHAT DO YOU CALL A BOX FULL OF RULERS?

A MEASURE CHEST.

How do you make a
duck trip?

- - - - - - - - - - - - -

Put him on an *airplane.*

WHAT DOES THE WINNER
OF A RACE AGAINST
STORKULES LOSE?

HiS BREATH.

WHAT'S THE
DIFFERENCE BETWEEN A
MUMMY AND A DUCK?

A MUMMY CAN DUCK, BUT
A DUCK CAN'T MUMMY.

What do krakens
eat for lunch?

FISH AND SHIPS.

How do you cut the
ocean in half?

With
a
SEA-
saw!

i COULDN'T REMEMBER iF
ZEUS'S POWER WAS THUNDER
OR LiGHTNiNG.

BUT THEN iT
STRUCK
ME!

DiD i EVER TELL YOU ABOU
THE TiME WE WENT CAMPING
AND BiGFOOT ATTACKED?

iT WAS iN-TENTS!

Not funny, Launchpad!
It was really scary. I'm trying to
FORG-YETI 'BOUT IT!

I still wake up
screaming at night.

WHAT DID DEWEY SAY WHEN LOUIE TRIED TO COLOR A TINY PICTURE OF HIS BROTHER?

"LOOKS GOOD, BUT IT'S A LITTLE HUE-Y."

THAT REMINDS ME OF THE TIME SCROOGE GOT HIS PORTRAIT PAINTED! HE WAS FEELING A LITTLE SELF-CONSCIOUS ABOUT HIS AGE, THOUGH, SO HE KEPT ASKING THE PAINTER, "COULD YOU PAINT ME A LITTLE YOUNGER? A LITTLE YOUNGER THAN THAT, MAYBE. YOUNGER STILL!"

THE PAINTER GOT SO ANNOYED WITH HIM THAT SHE WALKED AWAY FROM HER EASEL, LEAVING SCROOGE WITH A PAINTING OF JUST AN EGG. WHOOPS! THAT ARTIST WAS REALLY TALENTED, THOUGH. SHE COULD ALWAYS DRAW A CROWD.

What does the Junior Woodchucks' Guide say about **mummies?**

The same thing it says about **daddies.**

WHAT DID THE REGULAR TREE SAY TO THE COMEDIAN TREE?

Wood you cut it out?

That's acorn-y joke.

WHAT DO YOU CALL A WOODCHUCK WHO'S HANGING FROM THE TOP OF MOUNT NEVERREST?

CLIFF!

- - - - - - - - - - - - - -

What do you call a Woodchuck who camps right outside your front door?

MATT!

WHAT DO YOU CALL A SCOUT WHO LOVES THE <u>DICTIONARY</u>?

A <u>WORD</u>CHUCK.

I have to start looking for a new <u>Junior Woodchucks' Guide.</u>

But you just got one last week!

That's the one I'm looking for!

WHAT DO YOU CALL A SCOUT WHO LOVES TO **KNIT SWEATERS?**

A <u>WOOL</u>CHUCK.

WHAT DO YOU CALL A WOODCHUCK WHO FLOATS IN **WATER?**

BOB!

WHY WERE THE WOODCHUCKS
TIRED ON
APRIL FIRST?

- - - - - - - - - - - - - - - - -

THEY HAD JUST FINISHED A
THIRTY-ONE-DAY MARCH!

WHY DID THE WOODCHUCK
SIT ON **HIS WATCH?**

- - - - - - - - - - - - - - - -

He wanted to be
on time.

WHAT'S THE DIFFERENCE
BETWEEN A <u>WOODCHUCK</u>
AND A <u>BUSINESSDUCK?</u>

A <u>WOODCHUCK</u> TIES KNOTS,
AND A <u>BUSINESSDUCK</u>
KNOTS TIES.

What do you call bears
without ears?

B's.

Which **path** will tell you the right direction?

A COMPATH.

WHAT'S A WOODCHUCK'S FAVORITE PET?

A MERIT BADGER.

SCROOGE STILL HASN'T LAUGHED!

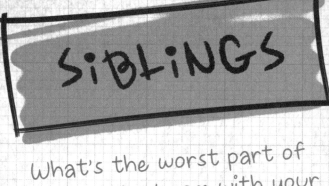

SIBLINGS

What's the worst part of sharing a bedroom with your brothers?

My brothers.

Why does your brother talk so much?

He swallowed a dictionary.

Donald wants you to help fix dinner.

Why?
Is it broken?

HOW CAN YOU TELL iF YOUR BROTHER iS TURNING iNTO A REFRIGERATOR?

OPEN HiS MOUTH AND SEE iF A LiGHT COMES ON.

Why does Dewey jump up and down before he takes his medicine?

Because the label says "shake before using."

Louie's a pain.

It could be worse.

How?

There could be two *of him.*

What happens to Dewey when he gets **cold**?

He gets <u>duck</u> bumps.

What has **feathers and flies?**

Louie, when he forgets to take a bath! Hey!

Uncle Donald, do you agree with the saying "Two wrongs don't make a right"?

OF COURSE! JUST LOOK AT YOUR BROTHERS.

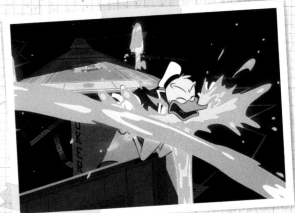

How do you make a

duck float?

Put him in a glass with some ice cream and root beer.

Who's your favorite brother?

I can't say, but you're definitely in the top <u>two</u>.

Why did the vampires lose the baseball game?

Their bats flew away.

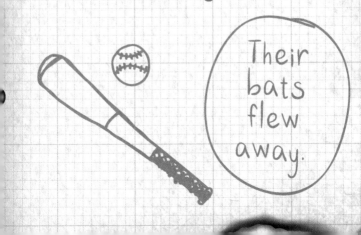

WHAT DO HUEY, DEWEY, LOUIE, AND WEBBY SLEEP ON IN THE MONEY BIN?

BANK BEDS.

WHAT HAPPENS TO A BROTHER WHEN YOU TAKE AWAY HIS R?

He becomes a bother.

WHAT DO YOU CALL A DUCK WHO LIES DOWN ON WET GRASS?

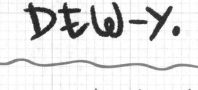

DEW-Y.

Who are the **best kids** in the **whole world**?

This joke is too **obvi-US!**

MORE JOKES TO TRY TO MAKE SCROOGE LAUGH

WHEN DOES SCROOGE WEAR HiS SPECIAL SPATS?

SPAT-URDAY!

What do you call Launchpad when he chauffeurs Uncle Scrooge?

A <u>Scrooge</u> driver.

WHAT IS SCROOGE'S FAVORITE FRUIT?

- - - - - - - - - - - -

HIS NUMBER-ONE <u>LIME</u>.

WHERE DOES SCROOGE KEEP ALL HIS JOKES?

- - - - - - - - - - - - -

IN HIS FUNNY BIN.

*If I had a funny bin, ⌐
these jokes would <u>not</u> be in it.*

Why is a river rich?

Because it has
two banks.

WHY WASN'T LOUIE ALLOWED
IN THE **MONEY BIN?**

HE WAS ON A
DIME-OUT.

WHAT DID SCROOGE'S
NUMBER-ONE DIME SAY TO
THE MONEY BIN?

"YOU HAVE A LOT MORE
CENTS THAN i DO."

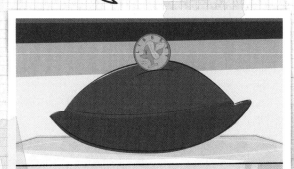

WHAT DO SCROOGE AND A
BAKER HAVE IN COMMON?

THEY'RE BOTH ROLLING IN
DOUGH!

WHERE DOES SCROOGE STORE ALL HIS RABBITS?

IN HIS BUNNY BIN.

WHY DOES SCROOGE WEAR A TOP HAT?

BECAUSE HE'D LOOK SILLY WEARING A HAT ON HIS BOTTOM.

I bet I could pull that look off, actually.

WHERE DOES SCROOGE
KEEP ALL HIS MANNEQUINS?

IN HIS DUMMY BIN.

WHERE DO GLACIER MONSTERS
KEEP THEIR MONEY?

IN SNOWBANKS.

WHAT WAS SCROOGE'S
FAVORITE TOY?

HIS DOLL-AR
HOUSE.

WHAT'S FOUR DIMES
PLUS FOUR DIMES?

THE SAME THING AS
TWO DIMES FOUR!

When does it rain money?

When there's change
in the weather.

Where can you find money whenever you need it?

The dictionary.

These aren't jokes. They're facts.

CRASHES

Why did you land your plane in a tree?

i THOUGHT i'D BRANCH OUT AND TRY SOMETHING NEW.

What did Launchpad say when he crashed into the broom closet?

SUPPLIES!

How does Launchpad enter a party?

He crashes it.

What do you get in your mouth when you crash in a desert after dinner?

DESERT.

Where's Launchpad?

He took a trip.

Where?

Right down these stairs.

OUCH!

WHAT DO YOU CALL CRASHING INTO A GARBAGE DUMP?

A TRASH LANDING.

How did Launchpad learn
to fly a plane?

He took a crash
course.

Why do pilots hate poison ivy?

THEY DON'T WANT TO GET A *C-RASH.*

What's funny about poison ivy, poison oak, and poison sumac?

NOTHING! SERIOUSLY. THEY iTCH LiKE CRAZY.

Why did Launchpad take his plane to the orchestra?

- - - - - - - - - - - - - - -

He thought it could use a
tune-up.

What kind of chocolate does
Launchpad love?

- - - - - - - - - - - - - - -

PLANE
CHOCOLATE!

What's the
difference between a
crash and a plane?

YOU CAN **CRASH** A PLANE, BUT
YOU CAN'T **PLANE** A CRASH.

Why did Launchpad crash
into the lake?

His plane was thirsty.

What's Launchpad's
favorite running event?

The hundred-meter
<u>crash.</u>

What's the hardest
part of crashing?

THE GROUND!

How is flying a plane a
lot like riding a bike?

THEY BOTH GET THEIR
OWN LANE IN TRAFFIC!

No! They don't!

THAT REMINDS ME. SOMETIMES I
GET OUT OF WORK BY TELLING
SCROOGE I NEED TO GO RENEW
MY "PILOT'S LICENSE." HE BUYS IT
EVERY TIME, EVEN THOUGH PILOT'S
LICENSES AREN'T REAL!

Huh? Launchpad, yes they are!
Do you not have one?!

What do you call someone who can drive cars <u>and</u> fly planes?

ME!

An auto-pilot!

What did Launchpad get Huey, Dewey, and Louie for their birthday?

NOT TELLING! YOU THINK YOU CAN TRICK ME THAT EASILY? HAH!

WHAT DID THE MOM AIRPLANE SAY TO THE KID AIRPLANE?

YOU'RE GROUNDED!

BELIEVE IT OR NOT, SCROOGE GROUNDED ME ONCE! BUT THAT WAS SUCH A LONG TIME AGO, AND I'VE MATURED A LOT SINCE.

That was last week, and I'm still mad you broke the fence.

NOTE TO SELF

STOP EMBARRASSING
SCROOGE AT FANCY GALAS
AND REMEMBER WHAT
THESE WORDS MEAN:

-HORS D'OEUVRES (OR-DURFS) = TINY
SANDWICHES. MAYBE DESIGNED SO YOU
CAN HONESTLY TELL SOMEONE "I ATE
TWENTY SANDWICHES TODAY!"

-CUFFLINKS = EARRINGS FOR YOUR SHIRT

-SPATS = STILL VERY CONFUSED ABOUT
THIS. HORSE SADDLES FOR YOUR FEET?

-MONOCLE = WHEN YOU'RE RICH, ONLY ONE
OF YOUR EYES HAS BAD EYESIGHT, I GUESS.

-CAVIAR = I DON'T KNOW WHAT THIS IS,
BUT IT'S SURPRISINGLY CRUNCHY. I SPAT IT
OUT IN THE LIMO'S GLOVE COMPARTMENT
AND NOW I'M SCARED TO OPEN IT.

-BIDET = NOT WATER FOUNTAIN.

-COLOGNE = NOT THE SAME AS COLON.

-POTPOURRI (POO-POO-REE) = POTATO
CHIPS SPRAYED WITH PERFUME. AN
ACQUIRED TASTE?

- THROAT LOZENGES FOR DONALD.

- THAT SPY NOVEL MRS. BEAKLEY WANTS—
  TINKER TAILOR SPARROW SPY.

- MORE THROWING STARS FOR WEBBY—ALL
  OF HERS ARE STUCK ON THE CEILING.
  NOT GONNA BE FUN WHEN THEY START
  FALLING DOWN.

- S'MORE INGREDIENTS FOR HUEY. WAIT, I
  CAN'T REMEMBER—SOME MORE OF WHAT?

- EXTRA-EXTRA-EXTRA-SPICY JALAPEÑO
  POPPERS FOR DEWEY AND LOUIE.

- EXTRA-EXTRA-EXTRA-STRENGTH UPSET
  STOMACH PILLS FOR DEWEY AND LOUIE.

- WEBBED FOOT FUNGUS CREAM FOR
  SCROOGE—AND ALSO THAT ROMANCE
  NOVEL HE WANTS, BEAK TO BEAK.

↖ Launchpad!!

That is _private_!!

SORRY, MR. MCDEE!
YOU SHOULD WASH
THOSE SPATS
SOMETIME, THOUGH.

LAUNCHPAD'S BEAUTIFUL MUSINGS AND DEEP THOUGHTS

IS RAIN LIKE A CAR WASH FOR YOUR LIFE?

WHY IS DUCKWORTH A DOG?

MONEY CAN BUY YOU ANYTHING . . . BUT HAPPINESS. OR MORE MONEY.

WHAT IS THE COLOR OF A MIRROR?

IS THERE AN ALTERNATE DIMENSION WHERE I'M UGLY?

DID MY PARENTS KNOW I'D BECOME A PILOT WHEN THEY NAMED ME LAUNCHPAD? ARE THEY PSYCHIC?

HUEY, DEWEY, AND LOUIE ARE TRIPLETS. DID THEY HATCH FROM THE SAME EGG?

WHY ARE PANTS CALLED PANTS EVEN THOUGH THERE'S ONLY ONE?

WHAT IS SOUND?

WHY DO WE ALL WEAR THE SAME CLOTHES EVERY DAY?

WHY DO WE ONLY HAVE TEETH WHEN WE TALK?

WHAT'S ORANGE, PURPLE, TALL, SHORT, AND ~~rev~~

WELP, i JUST CRASHED INTO MR. GLOMGOLD'S GOLDEN STATUE OF HIMSELF, AND HE SAYS i OWE HIM $50,000 iN REPAIRS. i'M CERTAIN MR. MCDEE iS GONNA BAIL ME OUT, THOUGH!

HAHAHA!

Good one, Launchpad!!

you *finally* made me laugh!